W9-BGM-313

The Tin Soldier

and other toy stories

Compiled by Tig Thomas

Miles
KeLLY

First published in 2014 by Miles Kelly Publishing Ltd
Harding's Barn, Bardfield End Green, Thaxted, Essex, CM6 3PX, UK

Copyright © Miles Kelly Publishing Ltd 2014

2 4 6 8 10 9 7 5 3

Publishing Director Belinda Gallagher
Creative Director Jo Cowan
Editorial Director Rosie Neave
Senior Editor Sarah Parkin
Senior Designer Joe Jones
Production Manager Elizabeth Collins
Reprographics Stephan Davis, Jennifer Cozens, Thom Allaway

All rights reserved. No part of this publication may be reproduced, stored in a
retrieval system, or transmitted by any means, electronic, mechanical, photocopying,
recording or otherwise, without the prior permission of the copyright holder.

ISBN 978-1-78209-462-3

Printed in China

British Library Cataloguing-in-Publication Data
A catalogue record for this book is available from the British Library

ACKNOWLEDGEMENTS

The publishers would like to thank the following artists who have contributed to this book:
Advocate Art: Milena Jahier, Bruno Merz (inc. cover), Kimberley Scott
Beehive Illustration: Rupert Van Wyk (inc. decorative frames)

Made with paper from a sustainable forest

www.mileskelly.net   info@mileskelly.net

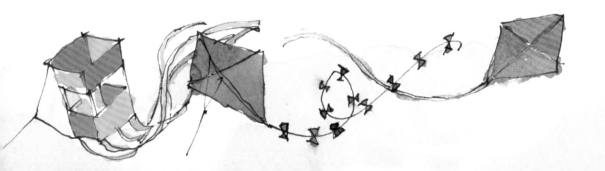

Contents

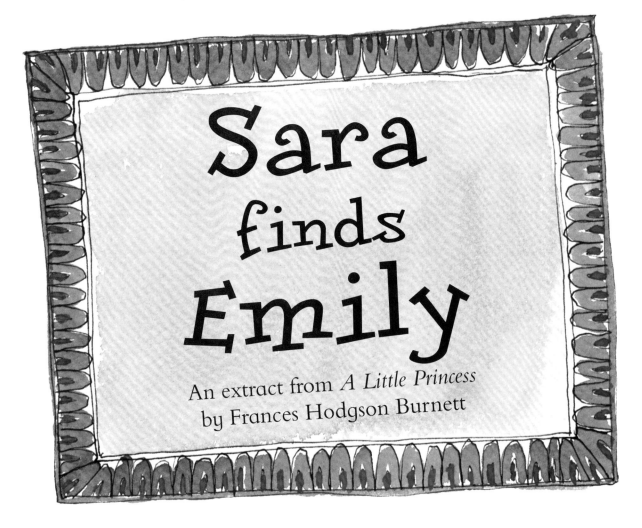

Sara finds Emily

An extract from *A Little Princess*
by Frances Hodgson Burnett

*Sara Crewe is being sent to a boarding school in London,
run by a woman called Miss Minchin, while her father,
Captain Crewe, goes to India.*

"**I AM NOT IN THE LEAST** anxious about her education," Captain Crewe said, as he held Sara's hand and patted it. "The difficulty will be to keep her from learning too fast and too much. She is always sitting

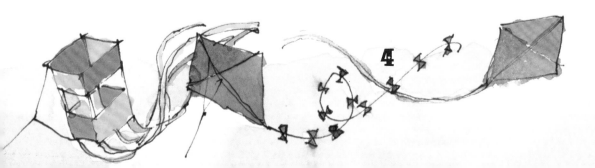

4

with her little nose burrowing into books. Drag her away from her books when she reads too much. Make her ride her pony or go out and buy a new doll. She ought to play more with dolls."

"Papa," said Sara, "if I went out and bought a new doll every few days, I should have more than I could be fond of. Dolls ought to be friends. Emily is going to be my friend."

Captain Crewe looked at Miss Minchin, and Miss Minchin looked back at him.

"Who is Emily?" Miss Minchin inquired.

"Tell her, Sara," Captain Crewe said, smiling at her.

Sara's green-grey eyes looked very solemn and quite soft as she answered.

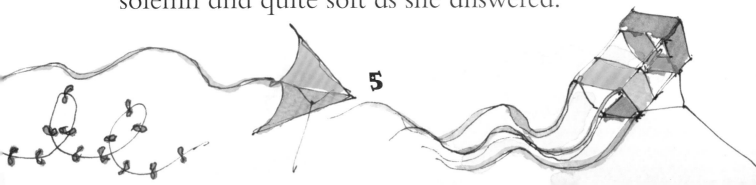

"She is a doll I haven't got yet," she said. "She is a doll Papa is going to buy for me. We are going out together to find her. I have called her Emily. She is going to be my friend when Papa is gone. I want her to talk to about him."

"What an original child!" Miss Minchin said. "What a darling little creature!"

"Yes," said Captain Crewe, drawing Sara close. "She is a darling little creature. Take great care of her for me, Miss Minchin."

Sara stayed with her father at his hotel for several days, in fact, she remained with him until he sailed away to India. They went out and visited many big shops together, and at last they found Emily. But they went to a number of toy shops and

looked at a great many dolls before they discovered her.

"I want her to look as if she wasn't a doll really," Sara said. "I want her to look as if she listens when I talk to her. The trouble with dolls, Papa" – and she put her head on one side and reflected as she said it – "the trouble with dolls is that they never seem to hear."

So they looked at big ones and little ones, at dolls with black eyes and dolls with blue, and at dolls with brown curls and dolls with golden braids.

After a number of disappointments they decided to walk and look in at the shop windows, and let the cab follow them. They had passed two or three places without even

going in, when, as they were approaching a shop that was really not a very large one, Sara suddenly started and clutched her father's arm.

"Oh, Papa!" she cried. "There is Emily!"

There was an expression in her green-grey eyes as if she had just recognized someone she was fond of.

"She is actually waiting there for us!" she said. "Let us go in to her."

"I feel as if we ought to have someone to introduce us," said Captain Crewe.

"You must introduce me and I will introduce you," said Sara. "But I knew her the minute I saw her, so perhaps she knew me, too."

Perhaps she had known her. The doll

certainly had a very intelligent expression in her eyes when Sara took her in her arms. She was a large doll, but not too large to carry about easily. She had naturally curling golden-brown hair, and her eyes were a deep, clear, grey-blue, with soft, thick eyelashes, which were real eyelashes and not mere painted lines.

"Of course," said Sara, looking into her face as she held her, "Papa, this is Emily."

So Emily was bought and taken to a children's outfitter's shop, and measured for a wardrobe as grand as Sara's own. She had lace frocks, and velvet and muslin ones, and hats and coats and beautiful lace-trimmed underclothes, and gloves and handkerchiefs.

"I should like her always to look as if she

was a child with a good mother," said Sara. "I'm her mother, though I am going to make a companion of her."

Captain Crewe would really have enjoyed the shopping tremendously, but a sad thought kept tugging at his heart. He got out of his bed in the middle of that night, and went and stood looking down at Sara, who lay asleep with Emily in her arms. Her black hair was spread out on the pillow, and Emily's golden-brown hair mingled with it. Both of them had lace-ruffled nightgowns, and both had long eyelashes that lay and curled up on their cheeks. Emily looked so like a real child that Captain Crewe felt glad she was there.

"Heigh-ho, little Sara," he said to

himself. "I don't believe you know how much your daddy will miss you."

The next day Captain Crewe took Sara to Miss Minchin's. He was to sail away the next morning. Captain Crewe went with Sara into her sitting room, and they bade each other goodbye. Sara sat on his knee and looked long and hard at his face.

"Are you learning me by heart, little Sara?" he said, stroking her hair.

"No," she answered. "I know you by heart. You are inside my heart." And they hugged tightly as if they would never let each other go.

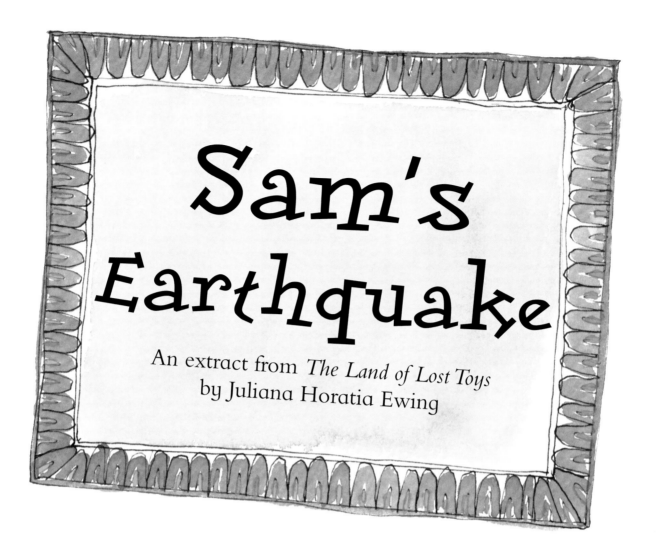

Sam's Earthquake

An extract from *The Land of Lost Toys*
by Juliana Horatia Ewing

SAM HAD ALWAYS had the knack of breaking his own toys. He also sometimes broke other people's, and his twin sister Dot was long-suffering.

Dot was firm, quick-witted and unselfish. When Sam scalped her new doll, and tied the black curls to a wigwam made from the curtains of a four-poster bed, Dot was upset. When she saw the hairless doll on the floor, she burst into tears. But in a moment she clenched her fists, forced back the tears and cried out, "I don't care."

Sam was sorry, and Dot was heroic and never told on him. There are, however, limits to everything. An earthquake celebrated with the whole contents of the toy cupboard was more than even she could bear.

It happened like this. Early one morning, Sam announced that he was going to give a grand show. He refused to share his plans with Dot, but he begged her to lend him all the toys she had, in return for which she was to be the only audience.

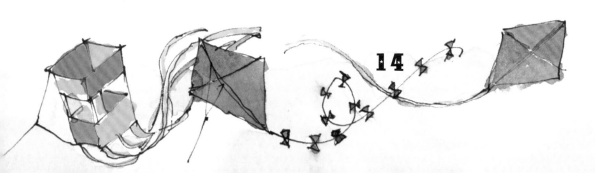

14

Sam's Earthquake

Dot tried hard to learn the secret, and to keep back some of her things. But Sam would tell her nothing, and he wanted all of her toys.

Dot gave them, and watched Sam carrying pieces of board and a green table cover into the nursery. At last, Sam threw open the door and ushered her into the rocking chair.

On a sort of table covered with green cloth, Sam had arranged all the toys to look roughly like a town, with its streets and buildings. It was not Sam's fault that

the doll's house, the farm, his own brick buildings and the cottages were all totally different sizes. The big dolls were seated in a building, made with the wooden bricks, and were taking tea out of Dot's new, china, doll's tea set.

Dot clapped loudly.

"Here, ladies and gentlemen," said Sam, "you see the great city of Lisbon, the capital of Portugal—"

Dot cheered and rocked herself to and fro in enjoyment.

"In this house," Sam said, "a party of Portuguese ladies are taking tea together."

"Breakfast, you mean," said Dot. "You said it was in the morning, you know."

"Well, they took tea for their breakfast,"

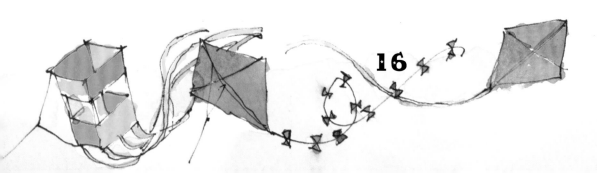

said Sam. "Don't interrupt me, Dot. You are the audience and you mustn't speak. Here you see two peasants – no! They are not Noah and his wife, Dot, and if you go on talking I shall shut up. I say they are peasants, peacefully driving cattle. At this moment a rumbling sound startles everyone in the city." Here Sam rolled some croquet balls around in a box, but the dolls sat as quiet as before, and only Dot was startled.

"This was succeeded by a slight shock." Here Sam shook the table, which upset some of the buildings.

"Some houses fell," Sam continued.

Dot began to look anxious.

"This shock was followed by others—"

"Take care," Dot begged.

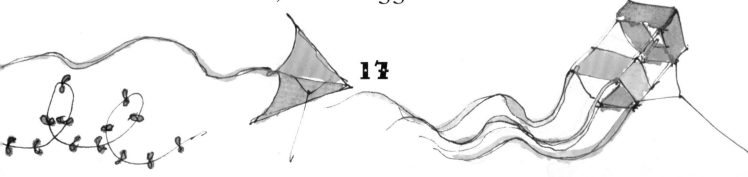

"—of greater strength."

"Oh, Sam!" Dot shrieked, jumping up.
"You're breaking the china!"

"The largest buildings shook," Sam said.

"Sam! Sam! The doll's house is falling,"
Dot cried, making wild efforts to save it.
But Sam held her back with one arm,

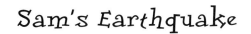

while with the other he began to pull at the boards that formed his table.

"Suddenly the ground split and opened with a fearful yawn." Sam jerked out the boards, and the doll's house, brick buildings, the farm and all the toys sank together in ruins.

"And in a moment the whole city of Lisbon was swallowed up," Sam continued. "Dot! Dot! What's the matter? It's splendid fun. Things must be broken

sometimes, and I'm sure it was exactly like the real thing. Dot! You don't care, do you? I didn't think you'd mind it. It was such a splendid earthquake."

But Dot was gasping and choking, and when at last she found breath, it was only to throw herself on her face upon the floor in tears. And Sam was sent to bed for the rest of the day. It was not until the next day that he came down.

"Oh, Dot!" Sam said, as soon as he could get her into a corner. "I am so very, very sorry! Particularly about the tea things."

"Never mind," said Dot, "I don't care."

"I have an idea to make up – will you help me, Dot?" cried Sam.

"What do you want?" asked Dot.

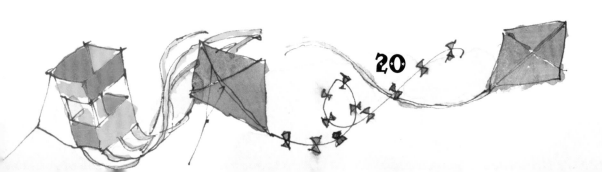

"It's the glue pot," Sam continued. "It does take so long to boil. And I have been stirring at the glue with a stick forever so long to get it to melt. It is very hot work. I wish you would take it for a bit. It's as much for your good as for mine."

"Is it?" said Dot. "What is the idea?"

"I won't tell you until I have finished my shop. I want to get to it now, and I wish you would take a turn at the glue pot."

By this time Sam had set up business in the window seat, and was fastening a large paper notice over his shop. It said:

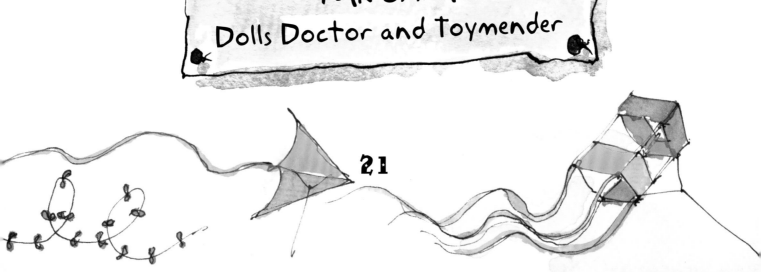

MR SAM
Dolls Doctor and Toymender

"Splendid!" shouted Dot.

Sam took the glue pot and began to bustle about.

"Now, Dot, get me all the broken toys, and we'll see what we can do. And here's a second idea. Do you see that box? Into that we shall put all the toys that are quite spoiled and cannot possibly be mended. For the future when I want a doll to spoil, I shall go to that box, and the same with any other toy that I want to destroy. I shall mend the dolls free, and keep all the furniture in repair."

Sam really kept his word. He had a natural turn for skilful mending, and looked after many a broken doll and chipped cup. When his birthday came round, which was

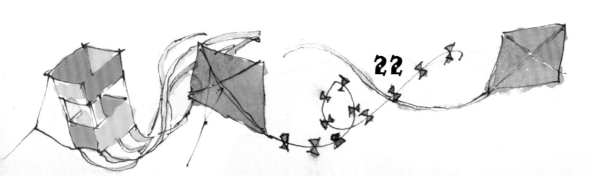

22

some months after these events, Dot (helped by her mother and Aunt Penelope) had prepared a surprise for him that was at least as good as any of his own 'splendid ideas'.

All the toys were assembled on the table to give Sam their present – a fine box of carpenter's tools as a reward for his services.

And certain gaps in the china tea set, some scars on the dolls' faces, and a good many new legs, both among the furniture and the animals, are now the only remaining traces of Sam's earthquake.

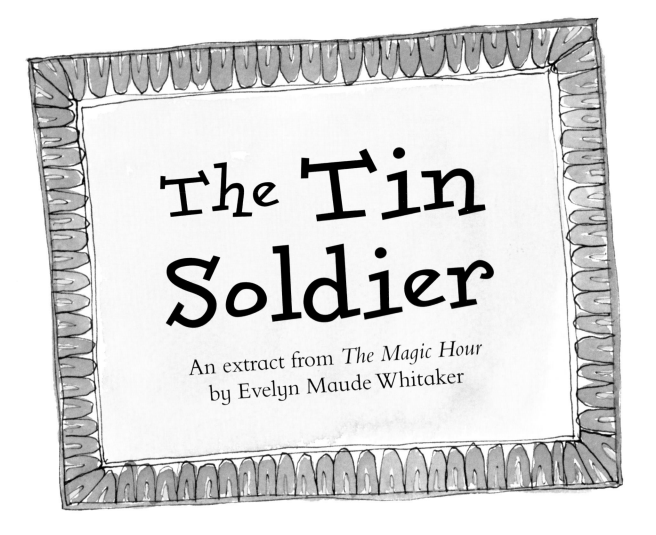

The Tin Soldier

An extract from *The Magic Hour*
by Evelyn Maude Whitaker

*Flossie has found a way to make one toy come to life every night
when she is in bed. A 'Tommy' is an old name for a soldier.*

FLOSSIE PULLED OUT a box from under
her bed. She leaned out and peered
down at the muddle of old scrappy things
that were in it – a pencil box, some marbles,
a tiny teapot, a ball, some bricks, a few

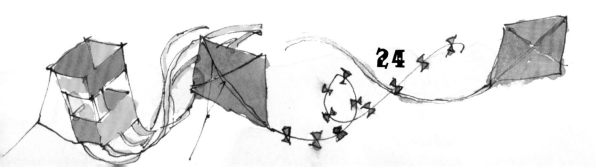

24

tiddlywinks, a whistle and a tin soldier.

Flossie stretched down and picked up the battered little warrior. She stood him in front of her and, for a moment or two, she was very thoughtful.

"Yes, I've decided," she said suddenly. "I'll bring the soldier to life and see what he has to tell me." Exactly half a minute later, the old tin soldier moved his head sharply.

"Hooray!" Flossie said aloud. "It's rather jolly having a real live Tommy on my bed."

The little man turned on her so suddenly and shouted so fiercely that she nearly knocked him over.

"My name isn't Tommy and I'll thank you to stop feeling jolly. There's nothing to be jolly about."

25

Flossie looked at him in surprise.

"What do you mean?" she asked, after a moment's silence.

"What I say," snapped the soldier.

Well, it was very bad-tempered of him to snap at her so, but Flossie took no notice and went on talking. "You see, my brother has gone to boarding school," she said. "Most of his soldiers are in the drawer, but somehow you have got into that box."

"Then why couldn't you leave me

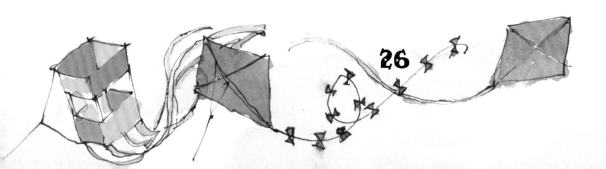

there?" asked the soldier in a harsh voice.

"I'm beginning to wish that I had," Flossie answered. "What's the matter?"

"I don't suppose you'd understand half of what I would say," the soldier replied.

"Oh! I think I should. You see, we learn all about battles at school."

The tin soldier looked rather pleased at that. He gave a very tiny smile.

"I'm very glad you learn something that sensible," he said at last.

"Do you like battles?" Flossie asked.

"Love them," he answered, "except when I'm an enemy."

"An enemy! How do you mean?"

"When I'm one of the enemy, I'm all the time being knocked over and pushed about

and treated roughly. I never get a chance to stand grandly in a row, or head a file of marching troops, and that's what I like best. No one wants to be the enemy, but, of course, some of us have to be, or there couldn't be a battle. But, you see, it's so horrid because you never win. Boys always make the enemy lose – in the end they are always beaten."

"How funny!" Flossie said. "I've often watched my brother playing with you, but I never thought of that. Of course, you are not often an enemy, are you?"

The little soldier leaned forward and looked into her face.

"It's a dreadful thing," he said in a solemn voice, "but the last five times that we

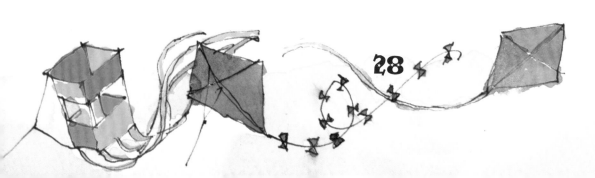

28

have been out, I've been one of the enemy."

"I wonder how that has happened," exclaimed Flossie.

"I've thought and thought," the soldier answered, "and the only reason that I can think of is that I'm a bit old and battered. You'll notice that my paint is off in several places, and I think Stephen very often has the shabbiest soldiers for the enemy. It worries me dreadfully."

His voice trailed away into a piteous little squeak, and Flossie leaned forward, looking at him carefully.

Yes, it was so! She could hardly believe her eyes, but it was so. It was so tiny that she could only just be sure that a tiny tear was slowly falling from the tin soldier's eye.

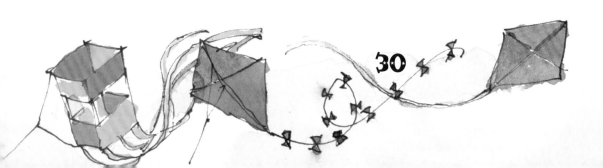

She put out a finger and gently patted the little man on the arm.

"You see," he said hopelessly, "I am rather battered and shabby, and now that I've been thrown into the odds and ends box, I shall never get back into the regiment. I'm almost certain to be thrown away before Stephen comes back from school. I shouldn't mind so much, if I hadn't been an enemy in my last five battles, but as it is—"

He made a little choking sound, and Flossie was so afraid that he was going to cry again, that she said hurriedly, "Oh! Don't make yourself unhappy. I'm sure I can help you."

"But how?" asked the soldier. "How can

you help me?"

"I'll tell you," she began happily. "I think I can make nearly everything come right for you again."

"But how? But how?" shouted the tin soldier, his face growing happy with hope.

"Well, first, after you have stopped being alive, I'll get my paint box and carefully make you look nice and new again."

"But will the paint stick on all right?"

"Yes, because I have some oil paints of Dad's. I can make you look ever so grand and I'll do it very nicely. When I have done that, and you are dry and ever so fine, I'll put you carefully back with the other soldiers in Stephen's drawer. You will look so fresh and new that, when he comes home,

he'll never dream of making you one of the enemy. There!"

Flossie smiled happily, and a shrill little laugh from the soldier rang through the air. "Ha! Ha! Ha! Oh! That's just fine," he said. "I'm sorry I was cross. Ha! Ha! Ha!"

He drew himself up to attention and suddenly marched forward, shouting, "Left, right, left, right." The tin soldier was going at such a rate that, before Flossie could put out a hand to stop him, he had marched right off the bed

and fallen headlong onto the carpet.

She leaned over and picked him up.

"Oh! I do hope you haven't hurt yourself," she said.

The tin soldier did not answer, and Flossie looked at him closely.

"I do hope," she began again, and then stopped. His 'alive' time had ended – the tin soldier was only a little toy once more. Flossie was sorry, but glad that he had understood that everything was going to be right again.

'I shall bring the paints,' she thought, 'and, when he is dry, I'll put him back with the others.'

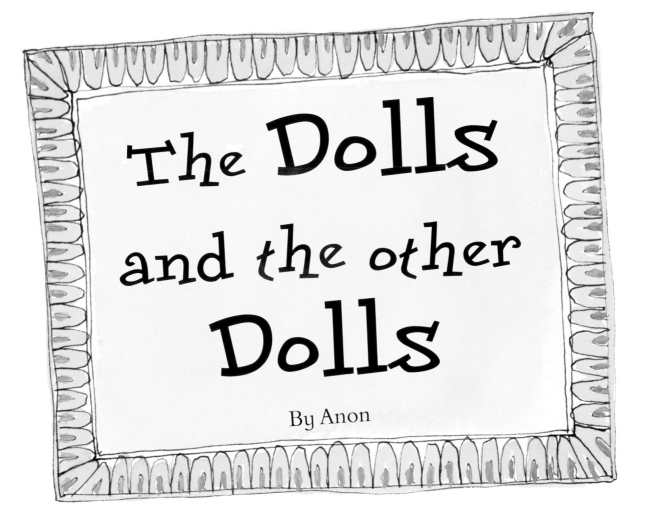

The Dolls and the other Dolls

By Anon

"**M**UMMY," LITTLE NELLIE ASKED, "is it all right to give away things that have been given to you?"

Her mother replied that it might be right sometimes, and she said, "But I should feel sad if I had given a friend a present and she

didn't like it, and was glad to part with it."

"O mother!" said Nellie, "you know how I love my dolls, every one, that my aunts and cousins sent me because I was sick. But now I am well again. There is an appeal for toys to go to the hospital to be presents for sick children. Some sick little girls in the hospital would love a doll. Would it be all right, if I keep only one of my dolls for myself, and send the other five of them for those poor children who haven't any?"

Her mother liked the plan. She gave Nellie a box, labelled for the hospital, and they lined it with some tissue paper, so the dolls wouldn't get bumped on their journey.

Then Nellie began kissing her dolls and laying them, one after another, in the box.

First she put in Lady Clarissa, who was very grand. She had long, curling dark hair and a beautiful white lace dress. On her feet were the tiniest, daintiest real leather boots that did up with teeny weeny laces.

Then Nellie placed in her baby doll, who sucked her thumb and looked as if she was asleep. Next, in went Alice, a little pocket-sized doll with straight brown hair and a suitcase. Then she put in Billy, her sailor boy doll with the cheeky smile. And then there were just two left, her favourites.

Nellie had always called them her twins. The two dolls wore white frocks and blue

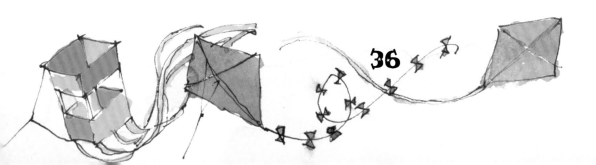

boots. They had real blonde hair, and their blue eyes would open and shut.

These lovely twins Nellie held in her arms a long time before she could decide which one to part with. When she did place one in the box, to be her own no more, a tear was on the doll's cheek (I do not think the drop came from the doll's eye). Her father carried the box down to the hospital, and Nellie watched it go from the window, holding very tight to her last doll.

A few days after the dolls had been given away, Nellie's mother let her invite three little girls to play with her. Each girl brought a doll, and the three dolls, with

Nellie's, looked sweet sitting together in a row. The girls chattered and laughed and made the dolls talk and hug each other.

Then Nellie's mother came into her room, which she had given to the girls to use that afternoon. She told the children she would give them a little supper of cakes, ice cream, pears and grapes, and it would be ready soon. All the children clapped and arranged the dolls around a little table.

As her mother went out of the room, Nellie went after her and said softly, "Mummy, I wouldn't take my dolls back if I could. I love to think they keep the sick children amused. But I do wish that for just a minute we had more dolls at this party."

Her mamma turned to her dressing table.

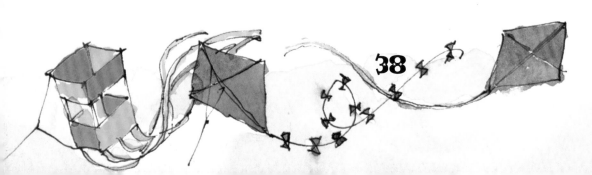

She put the four dolls in front of the mirror, and their reflection in the glass showed four more dolls!

"Five, six, seven, eight," cried all of the girls, delighted. "And all are twins – four pairs of twins!"

And so there were – each doll had her twin in the mirror, just exactly alike. After

supper they made the twins sit and stand, and dance, bow and shake hands, in front of the mirror.

So they played till dusk, when the other little girls' mothers came to take them home. After that, whenever Nellie felt lonely for her second twin doll, she would put her doll in front of the mirror, and together they would play with the other little doll that lived inside it.